Don't miss the other stories in the
Lollapalooza short story series:

Quarantine
Common Enemies
Coiled Danger
Mars Meeting

R.W. WALLACE
AUTHOR OF THE VANGUARD

MARS MEETING

A LOLLAPALOOZA SHORT STORY

BOOK 4

Mars Meeting

by R.W. Wallace

Copyright © 2020 by R.W. Wallace

Copy editing by Jinxie Gervasio

Cover by the author

Cover Illustration 27362914 © algolonline | 123rf.com

All characters and events in this book, other than those clearly in the public domain, are fictitious and any resemblance to real persons, living or dead, is purely coincidental.

All rights reserved. No part of this publication may be reproduced, distributed, or transmitted in any form or by any means, including photocopying, recording, or other electronic or mechanical methods, without the prior written permission of the publisher, except in the case of brief quotations embodied in critical reviews and certain other noncommercial uses permitted by copyright law.

www.rwwallace.com

ISBN: [979-10-95707-42-4]

Main category—Fiction

Other category—Science Fiction

First Edition

Also by R.W. Wallace

Mystery

The Tolosa Mystery Series
The Red Brick Haze (free)
The Red Brick Cellars
The Red Brick Basilica

Ghost Detective Shorts (coming soon)
Just Desserts
Lost Friends
Family Bonds
Till Death
Common Ground

Short Stories
Hidden Horrors
Cold Blue Eternity
Critters
Gertrude and the Trojan Horse
First Impressions
Let Them Eat Cake
Two's Company

Science Fiction (short stories)
The Vanguard

Adventure (short stories)
Size Matters

Fantasy (short stories)
Morbier Impossible
A Second Chance
Unexpected Consequences

MARS MEETING

Captain Arleen Kovak eased her ship, the Lollapalooza, into one of hundreds of docking stations in Mars's main port.

The place was bustling with activity; dockhands moving from one station to the next, making sure the ships were securely attached and lending a hand if necessary; dockmasters taking note of everything loaded and unloaded, checking lists and authorizations; various bots and machines doing the heavy lifting, transportation, and tallying.

Arleen had been flying around with an empty ship for too long—since the entire crew with the exception of herself and Yosu Gaal had passed away from a particularly violent version of the flu almost a month ago. She'd managed to replace the crew, and was well on her way to training them, but the cargo hold still echoed.

Mars would change that. One of the first planets to be colonized once space travel through worm holes had been discovered and made it possible to cover enormous distances in an unnaturally short time, it had become the largest shipping port in this part of the universe.

No matter where they were going next, Mars would have what they needed.

The question was what their destination would be.

Arleen glanced over at Yosu Gaal, sitting back in the copilot's seat, letting Arleen manage everything. His handsome face was relaxed, his jaw only working from time to time as he chewed his ever-present gum. Dark brown eyes on the docks outside the ship, missing nothing. Arms on the armrests, fingers relaxed on the disconnected controls.

Everything about him said he had no worries, no enemies lurking, no agenda.

Arleen knew that wasn't the case.

If he wanted to continue working with her, he was going to have to come clean. They'd already had one of their crew members try to make them all disappear forever into a wormhole because of Yosu and their mechanic, Anouk Roux. Arleen needed to know about potential threats like that so she could plan for them.

Or remove Yosu from the crew.

She really didn't want it to come to that. Yosu was excellent at his job, gaining the respect and trust of the crew in no time, knowing the ins and outs of space travel, and having a keen sense of business.

He was also kind, fascinating, mysterious, and gorgeous.

Would Arleen have made an effort to keep him on if he'd only been good at his job, if he wasn't also a friend she just might envision bringing even closer than friendship? Was she endangering her team by keeping Yosu by her side?

That was the million-dollar question she'd been asking herself since the incident with the communication centers, and she still had no answer.

It was also a rather silly question to be asking herself. Even if she did decide to trust the man despite his secrets, there was no way someone like Yosu would lower himself to being with her in anything but a professional capacity.

Arleen had one of those faces that could go unnoticed anywhere. Not too pretty, not too ugly, not too anything. Just an average woman who was incapable of keeping her hair in order for an entire day.

She ran a hand through her hair, feeling out her ponytail. It seemed mostly intact, with only a few strands running loose around her ears.

Yosu followed the movement of her hand with his eyes. The way they lingered at her neck probably meant her hair was in worse shape than she thought. Oh, well. No time to fix it now.

"You're confident the crew will be back here in three days?" Arleen asked as she started shutting down the Lollapalooza's systems.

"They'll be back," Yosu answered. He mirrored Arleen's movements on the copilot side, switching off systems and closing down screens. "There isn't much of a hiring market on Mars. And I told them I'd make it a priority to ruin their careers forever if anyone decided they'd had enough before the end of their contract." He gave a lopsided smile and winked.

Arleen's heart made a little lurch and she quickly told it to calm down, or else.

She brought up a map of the docks area on her personal tablet. "I'm not sure where we should go first. Last time I was here, I was just a part of the crew and had my three days off." She looked up to meet Yosu's eyes. "I think we should see what kind of goods are available before deciding on a destination."

"That sounds reasonable," Yosu said. He reached out and pressed the power button on the tablet. "But we have three whole days, Captain. Surely, you need to eat? There's a rather quaint Chinese restaurant at no more than a ten-minute walk from here—why don't we start there?"

Arleen's mind kicked into high gear immediately, picturing a romantic setting with live lights, low music, and Yosu feeding her his dessert, letting her lick his fingers to get every last drop of chocolate.

She shook her head, violently. Bad mind. Stay focused.

"No?" Yosu's eyebrows shot up in surprise. "You don't like Chinese? There's also a French restaurant here somewhere. I hear it's delicious, but quite a bit more expensive."

And more romantic.

"Chinese sounds good," Arleen said, her voice probably a little too brisk. "But we can't take all day. We have to decide on a destination before lunch tomorrow at the latest."

Yosu's smile seemed relieved for some reason. "Don't worry, Captain. We'll bring the work with us." His look turned mischievous for a second, forcing Arleen to tamp down on her imagination again. "You do know we can get all the information on that tablet of yours, yes? We don't need to physically go to every warehouse."

"I know." Arleen shot out of her seat, forcing Yosu to do the same, effectively hiding her rising blush. "But I'm not signing anything before I see the wares for real. Call me old-fashioned." She reached for the cockpit's door.

"You're not old-fashioned," Yosu said. Suddenly his voice was right in Arleen's ear. "You're thorough and take your job seriously. I like that in a…captain."

He was standing way too close. Arleen could feel his body heat all along her back, and his breath tickled her neck. How was he even at that height? He was almost a head taller than her.

Arleen couldn't decide if time slowed down, or if her body just wouldn't cooperate any longer. Her hand hovered above the door opener, as if pretending to want to push it, but never getting there. Yosu's body was like a magnet, pulling her back against him, tempting with his warmth and strength.

She was the captain here, dammit. Not some weak damsel in distress who couldn't even function whenever a pretty face came into view.

With renewed determination, Arleen pressed the button, and the door opened.

She stepped through, feeling both sad and relieved at the loss of Yosu's heat at her back. She glanced over her shoulder at him, where he still hadn't moved.

He blinked. Chewed his gum once. Cleared his throat.

"Chinese?" Arleen reminded him.

"Right." He took a deep breath and followed, pressing the button to close the door behind him. "Chinese."

☙

THE RESTAURANT HAD room for at least two hundred people. Arleen was relieved that Yosu's first idea for them to eat together was someplace that couldn't ever be described as romantic.

When her heart attempted to give its two cents, she squashed it down.

"Yosu Gaal!" the little man who met them at the door exclaimed. He must have some Chinese blood in him, but like with most people these days, there was also a healthy dose of other ethnicities. "You have come back to eat my dumplings. I had started to believe rumors not true, that you die with rest of crew. Why you not come eat my dumplings?"

Yosu shook the little man's outstretched hand with a rare genuine smile. "Chang, I'm happy to finally see you again. You are a sight for sore eyes, and your dumplings have been missed sorely, I promise. I will make up for it today, yes?"

Chang smiled from ear to ear, showing off a long line of even, white teeth. "Yes, you make up today. I bring four portions of dumplings."

Chuckling, Yosu gave the man a pat on the shoulder. "That sounds like a good plan." He squeezed before letting go. "Your English still not getting better, huh?"

Arleen's eyes shot to the little man. She hoped he wouldn't take offense at Yosu's criticism.

Chang let out a peal of laughter, a hand on his heart. "Good English no good for business, Yosu. You know this."

Yosu glanced at Arleen as he answered. "I know." The warmth in his eyes was absolutely mesmerizing.

Before Arleen could do something stupid and make an ass of herself, Yosu turned back to their host. "Any chance of getting one of the back tables, Chang? We have to work while we eat, I'm afraid."

Chang's eyes went comically wide. "You come with girl and you want to *work*? That is not right. Not right at all."

Clearing his throat, Yosu shifted on his feet. Was he blushing? "I don't think *girl* is the right word, Chang. And she's my captain." He shifted again. "We have to work."

The little man's gaze ping-ponged between Yosu and Arleen. "But... *You* are captain. You survive. Why they not give you new ship? You are *good* captain."

"Everyone might not agree with you on that one, Chang," Yosu said. The laughter was gone from his voice, and Arleen had the feeling he was communicating something with his eyes to the other man, something she couldn't see when he was turned away from her like that.

So Yosu had been a captain in the past? And something happened, making him lose both crew and ship? Could this have something to do with their mechanic, Anouk? And their chef trying to kill everyone only last week?

Chang got the message, whatever it was, and led them through the bustling restaurant, to a staircase in the back. On the second floor, the floor plan changed from the big open space downstairs to several large rooms with screens separating the tables, dimmer lighting, and fewer patrons.

They were seated at a table for two in the very back. None of the tables within viewing or hearing distance were occupied, giving them the space they needed to discuss business.

It was also decidedly more romantic than what Arleen had originally thought.

"What would you like to eat?" Yosu asked once they were seated. "I'm apparently having dumplings." His smile could have melted rocks.

A menu stood on the table, but Arleen didn't think anything would make much sense to her addled brain as long as the man across from her kept smiling like that. "I'd like something with sweet and sour sauce, please. I'll let the chef decide what meat to put in with it."

"Very well, Madam," Chang said with a bow. "I will bring wine."

Arleen opened her mouth to object, but the man was already gone.

"You can have one glass of wine, Captain," Yosu said. "You're not driving for three days. Who knows when the next time you can let go will be."

Huffing, Arleen grabbed the pitcher of water and poured herself a glass. One glass of wine probably wouldn't do any harm. And nobody would force the liquid down her throat.

"About the cargo," she said.

Yosu groaned. "We don't even have the snacks yet, and you're already talking business?"

Chang appeared, placed a bowl of snacks on their table, uncorked a bottle of white wine, and disappeared.

Yosu's expression could only be described as grumpy. It was cute as hell.

Fighting a smile, Arleen poured them each a glass of wine. "You promised we could work while we ate, Gaal. You've always appeared to be a man of your word."

He sighed. "Fine. You win." A sip of wine. "Let's just decide on a destination and decide what to fill the ship with accordingly. Mars has everything."

"All right. You have some specific destination you want to visit?"

Yosu had been studying her from behind his glass, but at this his eyes flickered to the left.

"Where do you need to go, Yosu?"

His expression hardened and he chewed his gum more forcefully than normal—a sure sign of strong emotion. He downed his glass of wine in one giant gulp, then set the glass carefully down, arranging it just so next to the water glass.

"Would you perhaps like to start by telling me about when you were captain?" Arleen softened her voice, but not too much. If he was to continue working in her crew, she had to know she could trust him. "Or how you were involved in Roux's father's death?"

Yosu's shoulders slumped. "So much for a romantic dinner. Fine." He blew a strand of hair off his forehead, then deposed of his gum in a piece of his napkin. Shoved two peanuts into his mouth instead.

"So." Arleen leaned back, her wine glass in one hand. "You were a captain...?"

03

Yosu hadn't just been a captain. He'd been the captain of a crew of fifty police officers, the youngest to be given such responsibilities since the creation of the universal police force.

He'd been good at his job and respected by the crew.

Pirates have been a constant problem since the generalization of space travel. Anyone with enough money can buy a ship, and the flying permit might be harder to pass than for a car, but not impossible. Once the ship is in space, it's up to the captain whether or not to respect the laws.

Whenever someone decides not to respect them, it's a real challenge to catch up with them. Because the universe is just so darn big.

Even with police stations spread out in all solar systems, in all parts of the universe, it takes up to forty-eight hours for a police vessel to arrive at the scene of a crime from the moment they receive the call.

Some pirates are stupid or unlucky and get caught.

Some, like Barberousse, Roux's father, are smart and play cat and mouse with the police for years.

The police usually do catch up with them eventually. Their technique is simple: they find someone on the pirate crew to bribe off, and once they have their inside man or woman, they can know in advance where the pirates will be and catch them in the act.

This was exactly what happened with Barberousse. They'd bribed two men to give them a heads up of where their next target would be, and Yosu had brought his ship in to wait to spring the trap.

"But instead of making a clean and silent arrest, everything went to hell." Yosu held the bottle of wine up to the light, seemingly surprised to discover it was almost empty. That's what happens when you down three glasses in ten minutes, buddy.

Arleen drew a finger along the rim of her glass, but she didn't drink. Her glass was still mostly full. "What happened?"

Yosu upended the bottle over his glass, frowning at the result. "Seems like I had a turncoat on my team, as well. He fired a shot, they responded, and then everybody died."

There must have been more to the fight than that, but there was no point in making the man relive all the details. Arleen would have enough trouble managing the aftermath of this meal as it was.

Chang arrived with their dishes and Yosu ordered another bottle of wine. Taking in Arleen's mostly full glass and Yosu's shiny eyes, the little man sent an accusing stare at Arleen.

She stared back and he went to get the wine.

"Did the police conclude it was your fault?" Arleen asked.

Yosu shrugged and bit into his first dumpling. His groan and blissed-out expression made Arleen's heart speed up and she couldn't help but wonder what other sounds he had in his repertoire.

She watched him enjoy his food, completely forgetting what they'd been talking about.

Yosu didn't, though, and once he'd finished his first plate of dumplings, he said, "I didn't stay around for long enough to find out what they'd planned for me. Handed in my resignation as soon as I could, took the severance package, and left. Couldn't take the stares," he added under his breath.

"They held you responsible?"

"Don't know." Yosu placed the second plate of dumplings in front of him. "Didn't ask."

"Did the turncoat get punished? Or was he killed in the fight?"

Yosu sighed like the world rested on his shoulders and poured himself another glass of wine. "The realization that he was probably planning on starting a fight is fairly recent."

"Is this the conversation our chef overheard, which caused him to try to kill us all?"

Wine glass empty. "That's the one."

Arleen focused on her food for a moment, while she chewed over the new information she now had. The chef seemed to have chosen chicken for her sweet and sour, but she had no idea what the different vegetables were. Lots of pretty colors, at least.

She set her fork and knife down on her plate and leaned her elbows on the table. "Now that it's been reported back that you know about the turncoat, and that you're in contact with the pirate's daughter, am I right to assume there will be more attacks? There's no reason to believe they'll be satisfied until they catch you."

"Kill me, you mean." Yosu was becoming downright glum, with his eyes at half-mast, his shoulders slumped and his lower lip jutted out. "And probably everyone I've been in contact with lately."

Arleen wanted to run back to her ship and call all her crew home. She needed to protect them, they were her responsibility. How could she look out for them if they were spread out all across this blasted red planet?

Yosu hung his head. "I can't put you in danger like that. I'll hand in my resignation." He shook his head slowly. "As soon as I'm sober."

That would be for the best. They already had proof that he exposed the entire crew and ship to danger, and she couldn't allow that. The Lollapalooza was a merchant ship, and not at all equipped to fight pirates—or police.

"Did nothing happen to the guy who shot when he shouldn't have?" she asked sharply.

"Not as far as I know. I think he also took a severance packet. Haven't heard anything about him since." Yosu ran a hand down his face. "Not that I've looked for him."

"Shouldn't an investigation have shown that he was largely at fault for what happened?"

Yosu seemed to try to think about it, but quickly gave up and poured himself another glass of wine instead. The second bottle was almost empty.

"There's a chance this goes further than just that one guy in the police force, isn't it? Where is it you'd like us to go next, exactly?"

Staring accusingly at his empty glass, Yosu leaned his jaw on his hand. It seemed like a slight breeze on his forearm would be enough to make the entire man fall onto the table. "Ekron," he replied.

The planet that had been handed over to the universal police force to use as headquarters.

"And were you planning on telling me *why* you wanted us to go there?"

Yosu's arm twitched and the balance was lost. He banged his head onto his plate, making the last dumpling explode, and his elbow slipped off the table, taking the glass of wine with it.

"You're moving on to water, buddy," Arleen snapped. "Then I'm going to have to decide on exactly how *pissed* I am at you knowingly putting us in danger like that."

ෆ

ARLEEN INTENDED TO sleep on the ship, but as they exited the restaurant, it became glaringly obvious that wouldn't happen. For one, Yosu was so drunk he couldn't stand up without assistance. That would make it a rather long trek, especially for Arleen, who was holding up most of the man's impressive weight.

Second, the minute Yosu was lucid enough to answer questions, they were going to *talk*. And doing that in a place where she could be certain nobody from the crew would overhear was clearly a good idea.

As she walked through the door of the first hotel she could find, she focused on those two points like they were life-lines.

She ignored the feel of Yosu's body against hers, his back muscles working to keep him upright, and his strong arm over her shoulder. So what if the mix of dumplings, wine, and man teased her senses?

He was dead drunk and not in control of neither mind nor body; not exactly the time to try anything.

Once they had a room, she sent Yosu into the bathroom to take a shower. "Preferably a cold one," she told him as she slammed the door shut.

Judging by the sounds he made as the water was turned on, he followed instructions.

Of course, just to make her life difficult, when he came back out, he wore nothing but a towel.

Keeping her eyes on his face and wet hair, Arleen guided him to the bed, and added a bed-full of sheets to cover the man up.

"Are you sober enough to explain yourself now?" she asked. She didn't want to get into the bed with him but stayed leaning against a tiny table shoved up against the wall.

Yosu nodded without meeting her eyes.

"What is it you plan to do once you get to Ekron?"

Yosu squeezed his eyes shut and shook his head, as if hoping that would arrange whatever messy state his brain was in. He touched his thighs as if searching his pockets, not that he presently had any.

"Start answering and I'll get your gum." Arleen slipped into the bathroom and found no less than three packets in the man's pants lying in a heap on the floor.

"Somebody planted that idiot on my team," Yosu said. "And told him what to do to maximize destruction. There's no way such a young guy could have known that *that* was the time to make a shot. It was strategic genius, and that just wasn't him."

Arleen threw one of the gum packets into Yosu's lap. Strawberry.

"*Thank you.*" Yosu ripped open the packet and shoved no less than three pieces into this mouth. As he started chewing, his shoulders visibly relaxed, his eyes became less tense, and he fell back into the sheets, making him look like he was only a photographer short of a photo shoot.

"Somebody set me up," he continued. "And I want to know who. I need to see the report—because from what Roux told me, most of it is not common knowledge, and that frankly surprises me—and I want to see if I can meet some of my old contacts. See if they've heard anything, if there are any other similar incidents."

Arleen played with the two packets of chewing gum she'd kept. Peppermint and basil. Who'd want to eat chewing gum tasting like basil?

"Why did you need to bring the Lollapalooza and her crew along on this revenge mission of yours?"

Yosu massaged his temple with one hand. "I didn't. I just... didn't want to leave you, and I didn't realize you'd all be in danger because of me."

Well, at least he apparently enjoyed working on the Lollapalooza, and their new crew. "When our chef tried to wipe us all out—you realized it was happening then, yes? So why haven't you taken off yet? Why are you still putting us at risk?" Arleen only realized she'd been shouting when she met Yosu's shocked eyes.

That didn't stop her from continuing. "Why were you planning to *trick* me into taking everyone to a place where we'd most likely all be in mortal danger because of our association with you?"

"I wasn't going to trick—"

"Yes, you were!" Arleen shot away from her position against the table and climbed onto the bed the better to shout in Yosu's face. "I talked to Anouk Roux. You two were going after whoever killed your crew and her father. And you were treating me like your personal chauffeur!"

Eyes huge and mouth hanging open in shock, Yosu whispered, "I'm sorry."

The fight bled out of Arleen. What was she doing, standing over a drunk guy in his bed, yelling at him for something he hadn't really done yet? She was the captain of the Lollapalooza; she decided where they went.

She sat back on her haunches, suddenly lost. Without thinking, she opened the packet of gum she still held, and popped one into her mouth.

She took one bite, then spit it out, right onto the sheets. "That's disgusting." Tongue hanging out, she looked around for a glass of water.

Yosu chuckled. "Basil, huh? It's a bit of an acquired taste."

Coming up empty on the water, Arleen instead opened the second packet. Peppermint took the place of basil, and the world was right again—sort of.

"I'll hand in my resignation first thing tomorrow morning," Yosu said, voice subdued.

"You'll do no such thing."

Yosu's eyebrows shot up. "But—"

"Then what are you going to do?" Arleen argued, vaguely wondering what the hell she was doing. "Go off with Anouk on a two-man suicide mission? What's your plan? What's your excuse for going to that place at all? I don't think anybody will believe you suddenly want to work for the police again."

"That was—"

"Yeah, yeah." Arleen waved him to silence. "That was what you needed the Lollapalooza for. But you can't just *use* people like that without asking their consent, you know?"

"I *know*. And I told you I'm—"

"So here's what we're going to do. We're going to figure out what kind of goods are needed on Ekron these days, and that's what we're going to fill our cargo hold with. Then we're going to have a long meeting with the crew to explain that there's more to this mission than just hauling cargo. I'm probably going to have to add in some sort of risk bonus for those willing to stay on.

"We need to figure out which ones we tell everything to, and which ones will accept the risk and extra money without questions. I'll leave that part to you."

Yosu nodded. He'd completely forgotten about his chewing gum, and it fell out of his mouth and onto the sheets in his lap.

"Is it a well-known fact that Roux is Barberousse's daughter?"

Head shaking.

"All right, we'll try to keep it that way, if Anouk agrees. Except the people keeping tabs on the both of you know, don't they?"

Arleen chewed on that as she chewed her gum. There might be something to this habit. It was like chewing boosted her brain along, somehow.

"Maybe she can go into hiding by stopping dying her hair pink," Arleen mused. "I'll have to check with her to see how she sees things, and what she's willing to do."

"I'm guessing she's willing to do quite a bit," Yosu said. The look in his eyes was reverent and Arleen wished his adoration wasn't just alcohol-induced. "She wants revenge on the guys stabbing her father in the back as much as I want revenge for my crew."

"Right." Arleen blew one bubble, just for the hell of it. "That settles that, then. Tomorrow, we start buying whatever the police on Ekron need."

Yosu shifted forward onto his knees, mirroring Arleen's position. The sheets fell downward and Arleen focused all her energy on keeping her eyes on the man's face and *not* check if the towel was still on.

"Why are you doing this?" he asked. He lifted a hand as if to touch Arleen's hair, then let it fall back down.

Arleen swallowed. Why *was* she doing it? "It's the right thing to do." Her voice was a lot less firm than just a minute earlier.

"But it has nothing to do with you, or your crew."

"It has to do with my universe. With the police who're supposed to protect us."

Yosu swayed but managed to stay upright. He might be over the worst of his drunkenness, but he was far from sober. "You could tell the authorities, if you really wanted to help. Tell someone whose job it is to go after two-timing pirates and corrupt cops."

"You could do that, too," Arleen whispered. Great, she was down to 'but *he* started it' kind of arguments.

"I need more information before I do that," he whispered back. Was he getting closer?

Arleen took a couple of desperate chews into her gum. "Well, there you go. Need more information."

He was definitely getting closer. Had Arleen allowed herself to look anywhere else that just at his face, she might have figured out how. "Why are you doing this for me, Captain?" His voice dropped. "Arleen?"

Arleen shivered at the sound of her name falling from his lips. Which were *decidedly* too close. "Why were you going to drag us all along when you could just as easily have taken off alone with Roux?"

Yosu's eyes flickered from Arleen's right eye to the left, then back again. Shit, he was *that* close. They dropped to her lips, then pulled back up. "Because I didn't want to leave you."

Then he kissed her.

☙

At first, Arleen was so shocked, she didn't even react.

Then the softness of Yosu's lips registered, and she couldn't help but kiss back. She was enveloped in the smell and feel of a strong and hotblooded man, and she was only human, after all.

The taste of white wine made her pull up short and separate her lips from Yosu's. "You're drunk," she reminded him—and herself. "You shouldn't do anything you'll regret tomorrow."

"There's no way I'll regret this," Yosu whispered as he grabbed onto Arleen's shirt to pull her closer. "It's what I've wanted since the first time I met you."

Really? He *had* to be pulling her leg.

When his attempt at kissing her again was rebuffed, he looked worried. "I might regret telling you that, though. You're going to take back your offer to come with me now, aren't you?"

"Of course not," Arleen said. Why was she still kneeling on the bed? Why wasn't she creating some space between them, so they had room to think?

Because Yosu was covered only by a towel—if that. And this close, she didn't run the risk of seeing too much. So there.

"Why?" Yosu sounded genuinely surprised. "I just made this horribly awkward. It'd be much easier to just get rid of me."

Arleen's lips curled into a smile. He was terribly cute when he was drunk and insecure. "It won't be awkward, Yosu. I just don't want to run the risk of taking advantage when you're this drunk."

He frowned as he worked his way through the statement. Then he lit up. "So if I wasn't drunk, you'd kiss me?"

Seriously, you'd think he was a pimply fourteen-year-old, not a thirty-something gorgeous guy who could smile anyone into his bed.

"I'm not sure if I should answer that." Arleen sighed. "It'll give you way too much power if you remember this when you sober up."

"Oh, I'll remember this." A flash of doubt across his features, then determination. "I'll remember."

"Tell you what. Why don't you try again at a time when we're both sober, and we'll see where it leads."

The intensity and anticipation in his eyes made Arleen wonder where he saw it leading. It certainly seemed to be an interesting place.

"I think I'm sober now," Yosu blurted.

"No, you're not."

"Yes, I am."

"Prove it."

His smile was blinding, then it disappeared as he threw himself out of the bed. "See, I can walk in a straight—"

Arleen just had time to observe that, no, the towel was no longer around his waist, and the goodies revealed were almost enough for her to change her mind on the only-when-sober rule, before he tripped over his own feet and fell face first on the floor.

"I'll leave you the room and go sleep on the Lollapalooza," Arleen said as she stepped over Yosu and toward the door. "We'll discuss the details of our new mission tomorrow, yes?"

Yosu grunted from the floor. "And when we're both sober, I'm kissing you again."

Arleen certainly hoped so.

AUTHOR'S NOTE

THANK YOU FOR reading *Mars Meeting*. I hope you enjoyed the story.

As of publication, this is the last story in the Lollapalooza short story series. But there will be more! The adventure continues as Yosu, Anouk, and the captain try to figure out what happened the day Yosu lost his team and Anouk her father. A fifth installment should be out very soon.

I also write in a bunch of other genres. You can, for example, pick up the first book in my Tolosa Mystery series for free on my website.

R.W. Wallace
www.rwwallace.com

Also by R.W. Wallace

Mystery

The Tolosa Mystery Series
The Red Brick Haze (free)
The Red Brick Cellars
The Red Brick Basilica

Ghost Detective Shorts (coming soon)
Just Desserts
Lost Friends
Family Bonds
Till Death
Family History
Common Ground
Heritage
Eternal Bond
New Beginnings

Short Stories
Cold Blue Eternity
Hidden Horrors
Critters
Gertrude and the Trojan Horse
First Impressions
Let Them Eat Cake
Out of Sight
Two's Company
Like Mother Like Daughter

Fantasy (Short Stories)
Unexpected Consequences
Morbier Impossible
A Second Chance

Science Fiction (Short Stories)
The Vanguard

Lollapalooza Shorts
Quarantine
Common Enemies
Coiled Danger
Mars Meeting

Adventure (Short Stories)
Size Matters

ABOUT THE AUTHOR

R.W. WALLACE WRITES in most genres, though she tends to end up in mystery more often than not. Dead bodies keep popping up all over the place whenever she sits down in front of her keyboard.

The stories mostly take place in Norway or France; the country she was born in and the one that has been her home for two decades. Don't ask her why she writes in English – she won't have a sensible answer for you.

Her Ghost Detective short story series appears in *Pulphouse Magazine*, starting in issue #9.

www.rwwallace.com

www.ingramcontent.com/pod-product-compliance
Lightning Source LLC
LaVergne TN
LVHW041717060526
838201LV00043B/779